I0608276

DEMONI VANKIL

HÖBIN LUCKYFELLER

EDITED BY
JAIME BUCKLEY

PERSPICACIOUS PUBLISHING

DEMONI VANKIL
By Höbin' Luckyfeller

Printed in the United States of America
First Printing: 2011

ISBN# 978-1-61463-124-8 (paperback)
ISBN# 978-1-61463-125-5 (hardback)
ISBN# 978-1-61463-126-2 (digital)

Perspicacious Publishing
1392 Turf Farm Rd #242
Payson, UT 84651

Second Edition
Edited & Cover Design by Jaime Buckley

CONTENTS

Dedicated to my children,
Alhannah *and* **Green**.

Run fast. Stay Free.
Record Everything.

CHAPTER 1
HOBIN'S DISCOVERY

As a fishis (Field Scribe Historian), you collect a lot of ...well, stuff. I collect more than most. That's why I'm the best at what I do.

In my rented room one night, I found myself staring at the towers of crates and packages — unevenly stacked and precariously reaching over my bed and small table. My eyes wandered over the field dates and priority numbers on each container. It was a system I'd developed to keep track of current work projects in order of priority. Filled with the knick-knacks of my adventures, each item held a story already written...or a story waiting to be discovered and told.

I absentmindedly ran my fingers over the surfaces of metal, wood, and heavy plastic — lingering at the soft woven cloth of scroll pouches. Checking the numbers, my memories worked their way into the past.

For some reason, I was trying to remember when this collection started. Reflecting on the decades of research and discoveries of my life, I located the medium-sized, faded blue 'smuggle crate' I acquired while at University. Scratches and dents adorned the surface of my very first piece of equipment.

I remembered one of my professors encouraging me to 'Be creative in collecting the data you may need.' Chuckling to myself, 'It's called creative acquisition,' they told us in training. The story you reveal may differ from the one you intended. Store away the dross until you can connect the facts and complete the puzzle.

'Steal what you have to', was what they meant.

My hand slid across the worn surface, searching for the hidden latch. There's a soft 'click' as the seal releases the false bottom inside the crate. Removing my old field journals, the letters from Sylvia and Alhannah's first hunting knives, I lifted the separator out.

Perfectly nestled in the bottom was a rectangular wooden box. A puzzle box made of a glossy red wood — sifterwood or manzanita from the grains. The crate preserved it well, the wood still polished after years. Except it wasn't new.

The box was already hundreds of years old when I found it.

I was working for King Robert III on my very first job outside Clockworks City. Morphiophelius had been insistent. The priests were inexperienced with Gnomes despite the job requiring a 'professional touch'. From their wide-eyed looks...I'm not sure they'd even seen one until I showed up. The Church was determined to fill the holes in their history and prove their rights of succession, and they wouldn't let any other humans on the dig site.

They found remains of an old kirk two days' ride from Castle Andilain. The kirk was the residence and service location for a Brotherhood priest during his vows. Administering to the poor and needy, caring for the widows, teaching the orphans...and when someone was at death's door, the priest would administer last rites and prepare a proper burial. His 'flock' were those within a two-day walk.

The Brotherhood's uniqueness came from their reverence for life. Ancient priests believed every soul had a purpose, to be remembered in life and in death. A life lived without acknowledgement would be an affront to the Gods. The priests felt it was their solemn duty to write about those abandoned souls — people at death's door without family or friends to care for them.

From a historical perspective, I can appreciate that. It was a beautiful belief.

It was common for priests to preserve their life's work. They'd hide their journals in hollowed out foundation blocks of their kirk before they died. The Church sought records with the priest's name and line of authority. The letters and testimonies about the 'flock', which the deceased priest wanted to be remembered, were ignored by the Church.

Unimportant. Discarded. Rubbish.

That's when I picked up the puzzle box.

The priests couldn't open it, and they assumed it was broken because it rattled. Probably just a loose piece inside, preventing it from opening. Thus, they discarded it and left it on the research table...in the *rain*.

So I put it somewhere for safekeeping.

Shaking it lightly, I could still hear the loose piece inside. Adjusting the cybernetic implant in my left eye, I scrutinized the box more. The craftsmanship was extraordinary. Evolu make, would be my guess. It almost looked like they grew the box from a single plant, the mark of a true master's hand. Almost invisible symbols hid in the knots of the wood, but I couldn't identify them.

These were new to me.

If I slid the carved shapes into the right combination, it should open.

Well, nearly a week and more than a hundred attempts later...the lid slid open. The puzzle was solved.

...or so I thought.

Contained inside was a set of letters. Fourteen neatly folded and stacked together, tied with a simple blue ribbon. Setting the box aside, I untied the bow and lightly examined the letters with the end of a pencil, careful not to let the oils of my skin mar their surface. The two top letters showed deep creases, light stains, and were slightly worn, while the other twelve were crisp with minimal wear. Actually, they looked as if they could have been written yesterday.

Fascinating.

I would soon discover that the answers to the greatest mystery of my career had been in my possession for decades...

CHAPTER 2
LETTER ONE

My Beloved Ethany,

I have arrived in Andilain unharmed and weary.

Now I know why you have always desired to see Andilain at this time of year. The sweet fragrance of the trees blossoming remind me of the soft skin at your neck. If we should ever travel here, I will insist on taking a carriage. You know how I detest riding horses and after two days, my back-side would be grateful if I never beheld a saddle again.

The trip was uneventful and my royal escort was not unkind to me, though their conversations haunted my sleep.

People whisper that the Dark Lord is closer to our home than I thought possible. The armies of Andilain, even now, wage war against the Vallen forces in the south, which have plundered the small villages of the coast. If these guards are credible, Mahan is a greater threat than I ever imagined.

Despite my inquiries, my guards were clueless about my summons. I have my suspicions.

They have given me quarters and informed that they will bring me before the King and Queen this evening. Being uncertain of what's coming, I thought it wise to send this letter now.

My love, I do not wish to alarm you, but it may be wise to gather the girls and visit Elaine or your cousins in Whitewater. My passion for magic and consuming curiosity get the better of me and I fear this weakness has now placed our family in danger. I never should have challenged the mägo. It was foolish and selfish.

I beg you to listen carefully and follow my instructions.

Pack only what you need for a fortnight

and leave the cottage immediately. Leave no word with your friends, only that you are traveling west to see your cousins. Instead, I want you to go north to Midell and stay with Aiden. I have already sent him word to prepare for your arrival. Speak to no one in your travels. My sweet love, I am so sorry for creating circumstances that jeopardized the safety of you and the girls.

All my love,
Eamon

CHAPTER 3
LETTER TWO

My Beloved Ethany,

I am sorry it has taken so long to send you news. Please don't worry, for I am safe. Thankfully, I received word from Aiden that you all had arrived unharmed, which comforted me. I pray your travels went well and that the girls believe this to be nothing more than a family excursion.

The six days and nights past have been much occupied in deep council. A neuvo-kuisa they call it. In this grand council, which High King Gaston and Queen Älodiä gathered, it surprised me to see that more than just humans represented. I recognized Kimmeldell the Bold of the Kutollum, the Evolu, the

Iskäri and even the reclusive Nocturi....and one other.

Of all the people to find, Charles is here. Just when you think you know your friend. He is blessed to claim the confidence of the crown and I soon discovered it was he that recommended me for this task. He shared my blighted history with the council even though the others of our Order scowl at me. No doubt they seek vengeance for my sacrilege against magic.

Ethany, things are so much worse than I have imagined. I did not see the shadow that hovers over the entire world. The Kingdom, our allies, the very world...is on the brink of ruin. Mahan has challenged every nation of light. Countless have died. Spy's report, the Dark Lord is now gathering his forces to wage his greatest campaign of bloodshed against Andilain. The hills of Äsä-Illäriu are aflame, the Holy City of Väthinerä invaded, and even now, the Evolu and Nocturi flee to our lands for safety. No race can hope to stand alone against the crushing blows of the enemy. The Kutollum to the north and our own people remain free...for now.

The Kings are fierce and none other that the Hero himself has enlisted us. It's our duty to put an end to this evil. But it will take great sacrifice. Not of money, but of life. What they ask has never been done, and it seems impossible.

As I first feared, the Council is aware of my experiments in the halls of magic, and that is why I am here.

Ethany, I miss you most dearly. You've always encouraged me and been a strength through the years. Your wisdom, your gentle counsel, would be of precious value to me right now. But here I must decide what is best for my family alone...and this is a most difficult decision. It has nothing to do with the nation, the soil, or the King's desires. This is about you, my beloved. It is about Saffron and Melody, and keeping you each safe from the evil that is approaching us. If we cannot stop the evil, it will surely find us.

I can help. You are the only one who is aware of my current project. They don't realize the progress I have made in secret and how much can be accomplished with the right help and tools. They need me, Ethany.

The war could be turned by the skills of a simple mägo clerk. So, I pray for your patience and understanding.

I could not protect you if I were to come home. We could run for a time, but the tide of war will speedily find us, I am sure of it, as it devours the lands, and then what? Where would we go? When darkness ravages and destroys everything we know, how will we survive?

The crown will dispatch a royal guard to you within a fortnight. They will escort you to our home that you may collect our belongings. There is a stronghold in the East, in Bailish. You will be safe there. The Queen has vowed to me she will keep you and the girls safe. Safer than you would be with me. This war will soon bring bloodshed to our doorsteps, my love. Only upon her solemn vow did I consent.

My dear, I also informed the Queen that you have experience tutoring in the House of Lords so that you may have means of support until I can return for you.

Listen carefully, Ethany—remove the floorboards under my chair by the fire and the second red cornerstone of the hearth.

You will find my journals and rune scrolls. Give them to the Captain and he will bring them to me.

Be brave, my love. I know it is a great sacrifice, but this is the only way. I promise to work with haste and diligence and to be with you before the snow falls next season.

Hug the girls for me. Tell them that Papa loves them and not to grow too much before I come home. Pray for me as I will for you.

All my love,
Eamon

Fascinating!

My first clue. High King Gaston and Queen Älodiä were two of the greatest rulers in human history. Gaston being the son of a human and Älodiä being the noble daughter of the Evolu.

I have a time frame. 5871s-6017s.

These letters are at least 700 years old.

Few records exist from this point in history. The documents concerning the great conflicts of the nations against the Dark Lord are written with bias, favoring the race of the writer.

Also, it was a focused tactic in times of war to cripple the future generations of an enemy by destroying their records when found. Journals, histories, church records, genealogies, anything that gives a person solid roots to build on and pass onto the next generation. If people lack accurate historical records of their ancestors, it becomes easier for others to plant seeds of false information. A nation can be polluted and undone.

Which makes these letters invaluable.

It's so hard to discern the truth until you can isolate common patterns.

However, there is one prevailing pattern in all the scattered histories of the races concerning this time period. Every nation of the world was in turmoil. Mahan was doing a sweep of the globe to either dominate or exterminate. His forces had become so numerous, he could control the field of battle by numbers alone—the war of Sharu, against the Nocturi, spoke of an army so vast, it outnumbered their own 300 to 1. In fleeing the field, scribes recorded the terrifying sight of the enemy falling upon the dead, rending them with their teeth and consuming them as food.

I read the letter again, my eyes halting when I saw

'rune scrolls'. I didn't know what to make of this at first. Really? Rune scrolls? Rune lore is folklore. I believe all lore is probably based on a truth somewhere. That's why I'm good at my job. Believe everything until you prove it otherwise. Anyway. Anything I have found throughout my career has been little more than children playing pretend with magic drawings or decrepit old bards singing songs of Runelords who all died of a debilitating disease. I mean, come on.

The dwarves tell more interesting stories of warriors who wore runes. Magic so powerful that a single armored titan could bring down an enemy's army unaided. Or that placing runes on their swords or axes allowed them to slice through stone unhindered. Or their enchanted armor empowered them to walk through dragon's fire without singeing a single hair of their beard.

Poppycock, I know. But they sure make the stories entertaining.

There's also been the odd heretic throughout history claiming rune lore is real but somehow all record of them disappears...or never existed in the first place...and therein lies the tales of rune lore being a dark and evil magic. Nobody really knows. Nobody really understands.

And *neuvo-kuisa?* I wasn't familiar with that term

and nothing came up on the Fishis Archive Database (F.A.D.), so I would have to dig deeper. Maybe hunt for the language roots.

This Eamon was at the center of that time, in 'deep council' with the greatest minds and leaders of that generation. Setting runes aside, it still lends credit to him. Which makes me curious about what experiments a mägo clerk was performing in secret—especially ones that would get the disapproval of his Order? The heretic?

...or just a clever loon?

CHAPTER 4
LETTER THREE

My Beloved Ethany,

It has been thirty-one days since I have beheld your lovely face and my heart aches for you and the girls.

I am told it is safe for me to send letters now, as we have finally arrived at the hidden place. Where none will search and nothing will be found. It's fit for dwarves, I'm sure, but not the likes of me. But I thank the stars that we have traveled safely, for it was a long and arduous trip. Our camp is so remote, I fear regular communications will be challenging. I shall write you faithfully and send my messages in bundles as often as the opportunity arises.

Oh, what I have seen during my travels, Ethany!

Dragons! True as the red in my beard, I beheld a full grown dragon near the winter foothills not more than a week into our journey. The beast was so large its wings blotted out the rays of the sun several times. My heart was pounding as we kept to the trees to protect the horses. As it shrieked through the sky, I started but the Gypsy in our party, Shiro by name, laughed at me before he explained it was a female in search of food for her young. That cry scared beasts into movement, providing her with a successful hunt. For Melody's sake, I had hoped to see a young beast in the sky, but my searching was for naught.

The Kutollum are a jolly people, my love, full of lore and hope for the future. Their leader, Hammel, is a soft-spoken dwarf and appears thoughtful. Being well versed in the history of their race, he occupied many tedious days with ancient stories of his ancestors. The most interesting being why they migrated north to the ice wastelands. We have some things in common. Hammel also has two daughters, of whom he speaks dearly.

A fortnight into the trip, we were unfortunate to travel through the remains of a ravaged Westgaiden. Someone had burned the homes and decimated the farms, leaving not a breath of life behind. A heavy residue of sulfur burned our lungs. I immediately recognized the signs of Täuku and their abominable craft—tearing at the very elements of nature to do their bidding. A terrifying race. It will be years before anything will grow. My mind agonized for you and I spent the rest of the day in silence, hoping and praying you and the girls are somewhere warm and safe. I am grateful for the vow of the Queen to keep you far away from the devastation of this war.

It's utterly cold and desolate here. In the evenings, I miss your warmth. I try to focus on the early morning laughter of the girls and the songs sung while braiding one another's hair. Your soft voice in the kitchen, singing to the rising sun. Each of your voices echoes clearly in my mind, bringing warmth to my soul.

I am confident in my assignment and believe it will go faster than expected, my love, and therefore I pray to return to you sooner than expected. Let the girls know about my travels, especially little Melody. I am sure she would be fascinated by what I have seen in the past three weeks. Oh, the stories I will tell them when I get home!

Kiss the little ones for me, soundly on the forehead as I would have done.

All my love,
Eamon

Täuku. Now, there's a surprising development in the war. I don't think I've seen the Täuku involvement recorded anywhere. There is nothing so vile or horrifying in this world than that damnable race and nothing, NOTHING I hate more! The lowliest of beasts and creatures should hunt, disembowel, and burn every wretched Täuku, so that they may tread their ashes under their hooves!

I digress. My apologies. Wanting to trace Eamon's steps, I secured a copy of an ancient map of Humär and began tracing from Andilain northward. It was easy enough locating the land where the dragons were, but there was no reference to a town called West-gaiden. So I searched for an even older record that told me Westgaiden was a small fishing village on the west coast.

West coast? That's also puzzling. I guess there's nothing like taking the scenic route. But a 3-week journey on horseback by an unknown route makes locating his end position sketchy. Maybe that was the point.

CHAPTER 5
LETTER FOUR

My Beloved Ethany,

It has now been forty-seven days since I last saw you and the nights seem to get longer and more cold. The wind has a purpose of its own, bitting into flesh and bone without mercy, but I see the wisdom in this location.

Worry not in my sporadic writing, dear. Remember how consumed I can get in my studies and work when the topic is truly fascinating to me?

It is a challenge for me to not share with you what is encompassing my every waking moment and I can not divulge too much, but this much I believe it is safe to say. *The Hero of the Gem has chosen each of us for a specific reason. Exciting and scary, I know.*

My first hypothesis is this: It is possible for a mägo to imprison all darkness using the skills of a Rune Keeper, a master of metallurgy and a Gypsy.

Now I must discover how.

Praying that you are all well and warm. Will write more soon.

All my love,
Eamon

Now, I really want to know what is Eamon up to.

I read the letter over again. Then again.

I have a time frame. 6000s, the world war against Mahan.

A meeting, a secret location—presumably in north-western Humär during the cold season.

The Hero, Evolu, Kutollum, Gypsy.

Imprison evil.

What could a mägo, a rune keeper, a blacksmith,

and a gypsy have in common? I'm really bothered to see the runes come up again. And a keeper this time. It has so little merit that it dampens my enjoyment of this story.

There is something here that I cannot put my finger on yet. I love a good puzzle.

I wondered if it might be the Demoni Vankil. I mean, the time is right. World events were pretty devastating and the unification of the races resulted in the defeat and capture of Mahan himself...and the use of a device. The darkest secret in history, the coveted mystery of all qualified and amateur historians.

No one actually knows what the Demoni Vankil is. 'Evil Chain' is as close an interpretation as anyone has discovered. Every attempt to uncover hints of its existence has trailed off into nothing. Zilch. Nada. There simply has been nothing to go on.

Instead, all we have are the muddy stories told from one generation to another. Distorting facts to the point, we can't discern between what's real and what's the embellishment of the imagination.

CHAPTER 6
LETTER FIVE

My Beloved Ethany,

Oh, how time defies us! I am constantly urged to work harder and faster. But the 230 days since I last held you in my arms have been so long and tedious. I keenly feel my absence in the girl's lives. I am beginning to forget the sweet scent of your skin on my lips and I count the days until I can hold you once more.

I wear your locket and the girls' bracelets close to my heart. It keeps me focused on my purpose.

It pains me I missed Saffron's eleventh birthday. We had plans to go to the spring fair this year and attend her first Father-Daughter dance. Please kiss her and tell her I was thinking of her, that I remembered, even though I could not be there. The cook made a simple cake, and we had a small celebration in camp to her honor, though I think Kutollum look for any reason to get out the ale.

My burdens are substantial, and a heavy ache grows in my chest. The entire camp waits on me as I, without a teacher, learn new languages. Test over and over the magical combinations taken from my journals...but my tests are too slow and meticulous in their tastes. They pressure me. They do not understand. Mixing the disciplines of magic must be exact. Even Hammel and Shiro have become exceedingly bored.

To pass the time, Hammel has carved a beautiful puzzle box from manzanita wood. He then had Renton forge delicate hinges of silver to hide within the twists and curves, corners and layers of the wood. I've never seen such skill or beauty.

Charles arrived this morning with devastating news. Ethany, someone murdered

Charles's family. Eva and the baby are gone.
Curse this blasted war! And curse Mahan!

Such sorrow weighs heavily on Charles,
leaving him broken and in need of time to
heal. I am concerned for him, as I too have
sacrificed for this cause. He will stay with me
for a time and assist in the experiments.

I miss you, my sweet. Painfully so.

All my love,
Eamon

2 30 days? I briefly glanced through the remaining letters, carefully unfolding them in order and laying them out. There are **tremendous** gaps. Where are the other letters? What have you done over the last 183 days, Eamon?

Of course, he will not give Ethany all the details—he's obviously hiding. He's working on a secret project. If anyone were to come across the letters in transit, it could compromise everything. Maybe even his family's safety. Is that why there are letters missing? Was it protection or deception?

It left me with a challenge: where do I look for the

creator of a prison? I started by looking into Eamon's first appearance.

It was difficult to locate any reference to a *neuvo-kuisa*. It wasn't a commonly used term by anyone. Only amongst royalty and those in a prominent position. This led me on a mini goose chase. Since the records of the crown in Andilain were barren, it forced me to find another option. There would be Evolu records. Normally this would not be the case—Evolu don't meddle in or concern themselves with the affairs of other races, especially political...but the ruling family wasn't just human. Lady Älodiä was from a noble Evolu house. That meant the elves had a direct interest in the crown's welfare.

I traveled to *Äsä-Illäriu*, the Evolu lands, and met with a representative from the Grand Library. Librarian Ainsley welcomed and encouraged my enquiring mind. They gave me a cot in the foyer, food and writing tools to take notes. Gotta love those elves.

He brought me a thick volume called the *Book of Three Shadows*, a history of events during the stay of the Evolu people on the human continent. Interesting title. I raised my eyebrows, hoping Ainsley would explain, but he only smiled and motioned me to read. I did so...late into the night.

The Evolu account of the war was something I had not read before.

Across the sea, the Nocturi and Evolu had driven Mahan's Täuku Invocators out of their homelands at great personal loss. Once fortified, the Evolu made an exodus from their homeland through the Prime Gates *'to join their human brothers'*.

To the west of Andilain, the Hero of the Gem attacked Mahan directly with a small army of elite human warriors, called the Nethinim. *'Men who refused to die,'* along with four thousand Evolu rangers.

'For we all feared the wrath and scrutiny of the Dark Lord...'

'...so cunning and intertwined in our societies were his spies that many trusted none.'

It was then that the Hero, through High King Gaston *'...in the utmost of secrecy gathered the wise and skilled to craft a plan. They would bind the evil that had thrust the lands of light into darkness. So decreed the neuvo-kuisa, the Council of Whispers.'*

Ah-hah. And there it is.

In this 'council of whispers', a name was presented. *'...a unique individual, charged with creating a method...'* Unfortunately, there's only a shred of information concerning him.

'...he held his head high, not with pride—but confidence. Only when his Queen pledged her protection to his wife and children did he bend a knee. He asked for letters of sanction from each race...then uttered a mägo oath to do all that was required of him...'

Sounds like a good guy.

Next, I petitioned for a letter of recommendation from the grand wizard Morphiophelius to take to the School of Magic. Surely, the greatest collection of magical knowledge on Elämä would have a record of a mägo clerk and experiments involving a magical prison.

Core, from what Morphiophelius told me, would be the logical discipline to engineer a prison or any spell of lasting containment. Traveling to meet with Master Caiden from the Order of Core almost proved a waste of time. Almost. Caiden was curt, arrogant, and unwilling to answer questions directly. He met me at the docks and prohibited my entry onto the school grounds. Morphiophelius's recommendation was the only reason my request to meet was granted. The letter never specified the interview had to be on school property. They're all warm and fuzzy, those mägo. Gotta love their literal interpretation.

Not.

However, I said 'almost' a waste of time because

his last statement in our somewhat heated exchange clarified my first hunch. He said:

"The School of Magic has a glorious history, which does not and has never dabbled in the pollution of its practices. We do not mingle disciplines other than a secondary language to support its primary. Those who do may not study at this institution and no longer exist to us..."

That is when I remembered Eamon's statement about being scowled at by those of his Order. He'd already destroyed his opportunities. Poor guy was destined for obscurity. He was disowned, struck from all the records of the Order, and forgotten.

He was on his own.

Mixing the disciplines? He would have had to study in secret and not expose himself. Brave guy, though. According to the mägo, mixing the disciplines is extremely dangerous, and one should never attempt it. Ever. I think it's common knowledge among the races.

This thrust me back into the world of myth, legend, and folklore.

I was doing a lot of running around without collecting a lot of information. I took a moment to examine the puzzle box.

Is this the very box Hammel carved?

Probably. I was right about the manzanita.

Where are the other letters?

And why would Ethany keep some and not the rest?

CHAPTER 7
LETTER SIX

My Beloved Ethany,

The isolation is killing me. The echoes and howling across this massive mountain range remind me daily of our remote location. It has been so long since I have heard your voice. I sometimes believe I hear it on the wind. I have not heard from you in so long and I believe I may go mad. I am tormented by the lack of any news...especially of the war. But I can feel it being waged upon our lands.

The supply wagons have become less frequent, and it forces us to rely on the wood lore of the Kutollum combined with our hunting skills to stay fed. Frost berries may fill a belly but do not satisfy for long. However, it's not the food that I miss so much as the news.

The last we heard, swarms of Vallen march on the western lands, laying waste to the towns and villages. I am told even the majestic Forest of Andle has been set aflame! Hammel has tried communicating with his people in the north by Artic Tern, but even he receives little news.

My progress is slow but steady. Even as I write, a renewed fire is kindled in my belly to complete this project in haste. I have the ability and knowledge to change our fate. I must succeed.

Pray for me Ethany. Pray for my speedy success. Pray for my sanity to sustain me through the nights while I pray for news.

All my love,
Eamon

The letters had consumed my every waking hour, and I made the tired, foolish mistake of taking them down to the tavern. Wood, the tavern keeper, brought me spiced roots and meats with a large pitcher of Blackseed Ale. I combed over each document by candlelight, seated near the popping fire.

Vallen patrons shouted and growled at one another in the tavern's background. In the corner, a priest of the Brotherhood was alone, sipping new wine and a small book, while old Terrin sang his tales at the hearth.

The mists in lands not far away,
Have hidden the deer and doe,
But alas, its power cannot hide,
The broken hearts and woe.

For upon the field of battle near,
Were waged the wars of shadow,
When men and elves and dwarves did fear,
The dead upon the meadows.

Choose ye this day, to serve darkness or light,
For the worth of a soul is revealed in the fight.

The evil swept across the sea.
And turned the days to night.
While wives and children fled the land,

Their men remained to fight.

The battle sore and blood did flow,
As many lost their lives,
The Vallen horde did pierce the lines,
With sword and lance and knives.

Choose ye this day, to serve darkness or light,
For the worth of a soul is revealed in the fight.

In the end the Gods did hear,
The cries of faithful men,
Who gave their all and fought with might,
Unto a bitter end.

For light did prick the night again,
The horde destroyed no more,
Now heroes live by bards abroad,
Their deeds are now our lore.

Choose ye this day, to serve darkness or light,
For the worth of a soul is revealed in the fight.

That old codger needs a new job—his music depresses the crap outta me.

Apparently the Vallen scum felt the same way, because the next thing I knew, a large metal mug filled with ale ricocheted off the hearth and onto my table. Black liquid sprayed over the whole of my notes... including the letters.

I bolted.

Standing up too quickly, I knocked over the candles I was reading by and ignited the drenched papers altogether. It suddenly engulfed the table in flames.

Beating the fire with my cloak, Wood finally doused the table with water as I felt back into my chair, horrified. In an instant, I had destroyed all the letters!

Pushing through the soggy ashes of my notes...I gasped.

Under the destroyed remains of my personal notebook were the 14 letters...unharmed! Lifting a single letter from the debris, the ash diluted ale beaded and rolled off the surface of the paper, leaving it dry and unblemished.

Lifting each letter, the result was the same. It harmed none of them in the slightest fashion. Peering at them more closely, I noticed a slight shimmer in the upper right corner of the paper. A small watermark. So they weren't completely indestructible. The impressive discovery made me more curious. Checking each page, I recognized a similar mark in the upper right corner. That wasn't an accident.

What I did next, I can't fully explain, because it was nothing more than a hunch.

Lighting one candle...I held the letter over the open flame.

The candle went out.

I lit a match and tried to hold it under the paper.

The match went out.

...so I set all the letters down on the table and poured the remains of my ale onto its center, then lit it on fire.

Wood hollered at me, but without taking my eyes from the flame, I assured him all was well and we both watched the fire consume the liquid in full and fade to nothing.

The table was unharmed...and so were the letters.

My conclusion is that rune lore is real.

And Eamon is possibly a genius.

CHAPTER 8
LETTER SEVEN

My Beloved Ethany,

I hoped, I searched, I desired. But now I know...rune lore is real! Oh, Ethany, the Order thought I was insane and mocked me, but never again. rune lore has proven itself to be all I had imagined and more.

The magic system's straightforward manifestations led to its demise and mythical status. Unfit for the great mägo Order, I've no doubt. But for me Ethany, brimming with possibilities!

The ancients never tapped into its full potential. Maybe they could not see the boundless power they beheld or else why would they allow it to fade into myth? It saddens me, this act of indolence. But do you know what this means, my love? I am that much closer to finishing my work and coming home!

We sought a method for bringing a rune to life. In this, Hammel has been indispensable. He alone, the keeper of ancient texts and runes, discovered a reference to 'Oro-Lifsin' or words of life. Combining the lore that says the first language had intent, life, if you will, and was binding, I knew we were bridging the gap into my expertise: languages. More specifically, the languages of the Seven Disciplines.

You may be wide-eyed and concerned, dear, with your hand covering your beautiful mouth, but I assure you, everything is well.

My skill was once considered reckless, unclear, and unpredictable, but now I have mastered it and no other mägo had imagined it before. I have successfully combined three of the seven languages into one powerful language and the result is life. The runes live!

I may have said too much, but my work will be known when you receive this letter. It is my fondest desire to return home to you and the girls before another holiday should pass beyond our reach.

King Kimmeldell arrived today with a fresh party of stout dwarven warriors. As a neuvo-kuisa representative, he asked for a progress update. His comprehension surprised me as I expected to find it necessary to simplify my explanations, but it wasn't so. Familiarity with rune lore may have fueled his imagination for possibilities. He seemed exceedingly pleased with our progress and gave us all encouragement.

I compiled a book of sketches for Melody's birthday that depicted the beautiful places and fascinating animals I have seen. She was growing fast when I left. She must be tall now. Please give the girls my love and tell them I miss them. I always miss them.

And you.

All my love,
Eamon

I t's real.

Rune lore actually exists.

Thanks to Eamon, I had proof that Rune lore is real, unlike the world that relies on stories from mothers and drunken Kutollum. Why is this magic form not recorded? In thirty years, I have searched the archives of gnomes, humans, Evolu, the ruins of the Nocturi. I've even interviewed my dear friends in Holääfeldi for some sign of rune lore, and every time, I came up empty.

Did the races conspire to keep this knowledge from the general populace?

And if so, why?

And who is this Hammel? A Kutollum Rune Keeper? Are the Kutollum keeping information to themselves? King Kimmeldell wasn't surprised by the rune progress presented by Eamon.

I think that is quite an accomplishment for 367 days of dedicated service.

CHAPTER 9
LETTER EIGHT

My Beloved Ethany,

I am weary. My red hair has turned ashen, and I am compelled to grip a cane with gnarled fingers as I walk. Will you still love me when you see me, my beloved? Will you see in my eyes the man who adores you, the same young man you fell in love with under the cottonwood trees that spring morning by the brook?

If I had known. If only I had some way of knowing before these experiments, I would have prevented this.

Rune lore is dangerous. To be a power that can work independently of its creator, a rune needs a life force to function. A literal life force.

The effects of our work were not immediately noticeable. I thought at first the change in my stature and the lightening of my beard and hair was because of the demanding rigors of this project. It was not.

Every experiment I have taken part in has taken a part of my life, Ethany. Drained it from my very soul to power the rune. I am not the only one. I see the effects on Shiro and Hammel, too. Hammel is affected least of all. The life of a Kutollum lasts hundreds of years, but he still feels the effects. Shiro and I have not been so fortunate.

This discovery has slowed our progress a great deal, though we press onward to our goal. We must stop Mahan.

I find my mind often wanders back to the day we met. I hope, my beloved, that you remember my heart and devotion, if not the youth of my face.

All my love,
Eamon

D o people not see the importance of keeping accurate records? Another 314 days passed. Now rune lore is dangerous? I feel as if I am getting too emotionally involved in Eamon's progress and the missing information grates on my nerves.

I have concluded it must be the Demoni Vankil he is working on. I have no solid proof, just a gut feeling.

The races all share the same two things: they don't know what the Demoni Vankil is, but they know it's the greatest triumph in history - the banishment of the Dark Lord! A singular event that created the Dragon's Chasm nearly rending Humär in two,...but sending the evil races scurrying back to their own lands. It brought peace, happiness, and prosperity back into the world.

CHAPTER 10
LETTER NINE

My Beloved Ethany,

709 days I have been gone and I cannot see the light at the end of this path. A growing fear within me whispers that I have made a grave error in judgement.

Have I pursued the wrong path? Is failure my destination after all this distance?

The draw of the runes is overwhelming. I couldn't imagine they would need so much life from a single source to function properly.

We cannot ask Hammel for another sacrifice, as it has weakened his life force. Despite the willingness of each Kutollum miner to give themselves to this cause, our camp is now a community of old men, and we've achieved nothing. It is not enough.

Shiro tells me he has an alternative, but the cost would be great. Greater than what we have already given? I don't know.

Have I failed after all this time?

I could use your wisdom now. You always have the right words when I'm feeling lost. I miss resting my head upon your soft breast. Listening as the beat of your heart pumps warm vitality throughout your body. Twirling your fingers in my hair, whispering your encouraging, soothing words and ideas.

I dwell upon the memories of our picnics by the stream — the girls playing on the grass — giggling as they chase butterflies.

Life has new meaning for me. I didn't realize how precious it was until this war consumed much of it.

Maybe I have missed something? Surely there must be an answer. A means to rewrite the intent in the rune or reshape the magic flow...

I will write again soon, my beloved. Do you still pray for me?

All my love,
Eamon

I didn't make the connection at first. Shiro is a Gypsy. That means he's an Iskäri—just not blue like the major colony. I may be wrong, but I don't think so. I should have noticed this sooner—because I live among the Gypsies.

Here in the Black Market, the Gypsies rule.

Some rules can be predicted but are not significant. It is the penalty for disobedience that is interesting. Breaking the rules can lead to a fine, prison time, or banishment for lighter races like Human, Gnome, Iskäri, Gypsy, Kutollum, or Evolu.

If, however, you're a Vallen—they pay the penalty with life. ...and it's a horrible sight to behold.

The Gypsies figured out how to drain life from others. Can't say I know much about it, other than having watched it first hand, once. The Gypsies are pretty public about punishment—making sure they make a powerful impression upon anyone looking to cause trouble.

The victim ends up a dry husk...or dust. The life force's destination was always a mystery to me.

What are Eamon and Shiro doing? and to whom are they doing it?

CHAPTER 11

LETTER TEN

My Beloved Ethany,

    King Kimmeldell returned two days back to look upon our progress and impress upon us the necessity of bringing these trials to fulfillment in haste. He brought disturbing news about the war. The darkness has spread across the coast and will soon reach Vänkiläsä. We are no longer safe. He has orders to move us and as quietly as possible. Should the Vallen slaves escape, they would be our undoing.

    The talent of the Gypsies has proven to be the salvation of our research. Shiro worked through the night to capture the remaining life force of the beasts. The screams were almost unbearable, but he was unerring on this. Vallen are strong in body and spirit, and the runes don't know the difference between good and evil. Unfortunately, we don't possess enough crystals to store all the life force, and many had to be put down by the blade. What a waste.

Much of what I write will not make sense to you, I'm sure. I find it difficult to separate myself from this work. I fear it possesses me.

A young human courier of the Kings has just arrived with dreadful news. Alas, Vänkiläsä is no more. She reminds me of you. It's her green eyes, the same as yours, and when she smiled in greeting, my heart stopped. It is hard not to let the wind here freeze your very hopes. I spend my nights sketching pictures of you and the girls and talking with them as if you were here.

But, you are not...and in the end, I miss you more.

Do you remember I do this for you? For Saffron and my darling Melody? Have they *grown much? Are they as lovely as their mother?*

We move in great haste now. They say the only haven left is deep within the very caves of Holääfeldi itself. I am grateful that we will no longer isolate ourselves.

Beloved, I would give another decade of my life to a rune for a moment to hold you in my arms again. To feel the warmth of your sweet breath upon my face and taste the tender sweetness of your kiss.

All my love,
Eamon

VANKILÄSÄ!!?

I tore through my crates, searching through the dates until I found a small metal container with rounded corners. Pushing the lock sequence, the lid popped open to reveal a small cloth scroll, and I had to smile.

Miracle number three. Sitting in front of me was another missing puzzle piece I'd possessed for over six years.

Field Entry, CT-709:2-11

I had developed strong friendships with the Kutollum Historians of the North. They share their history with those seeking to shine a favorable light upon the Dwarves. They are a great and noble people and when there is a shred of history which crosses their path, chances are, they'll have a record of it in some form.

So I had ventured north. My hopes were for discovering a certain genealogy line of a famous Nethinim. Someone with an obscure past, claiming to have been raised by the Kutollum.

With the permission of Lord Coldham, the primary historian of the Kutollum, I searched the dwarves's records for months. I could not find any trace of this human visiting, staying or learning from this stout race of warriors. After a month in the north country, frustration set in—the trail had gone cold.

What was I doing, chasing ghosts of the past that didn't want to be found?

The very beat of my heart told me this was more than a historical puzzle. It was a cry from the grave. A plea to be remembered for all the sacrifices made in blood.

I retraced my steps and go back to Humär to retrieve my primary records.

My travels took me down through the frozen wastelands of Ambasere, the kingdom of the noble King Borislav. It had been years since I traveled through his lands, when the people of the local villages sent word that a Gnome was in their lands. They soon invited me to the palace in Glaserte to dine with the Winter Wolf himself.

When questioned about my journey, I relayed the previous season of research. King Borislav seemed very interested in my quest and listened. Mentioning my thoughts about the lives of warriors needing to be told, the king smiled. He then dismissed his guards from the hall, poured two glasses of his famous crystal wine, and leaned forward.

"I have much to show you," he whispered, even though we were alone. "I must believe your plans have now changed."

...and he was right. The next day King Borislav met me at the castle gates with a dozen hunters, a cook, supplies and sleds roped to giant wolves. He insisted I accompany him on an expedition: a two-day ride west.

If you've never ridden in a sled pulled by wolves the size of bears...I don't recommend it. The trees and scenery whipped by as we leaped across the frozen landscape, whistles steering the wolf trains as whips cracked from the hunter's hand. They had to strap my body to the sled for fear of me falling by the wayside or bouncing off and breaking my body against a tree.

We passed the Prime Gate in the Ochra-Ruce mountains before the sun set on the first day. I'd never traveled that far west, and not in such a short time. The forests become dense and unforgiving unless you have considerable wilderness skills or wood lore, to which I had neither. We were rarely disturbed by the predators of the forest because Borislav and his men communicated with them.

Food was abundant, as was strong drink, so I can't complain. The night was loud with songs of victorious battles as fires blazed until dawn.

Just before nightfall the next day, our journey ended at the base of a sheer mountain range—a wall of ice and stone impassable. Fingers of ice was the name given to them by the trappers and natives, or the 'Sormi-jaa' as they called them. The ridge was persistently pounded by the wind, resulting in thick layers of ice that would not fully melt in warmer months.

The men started unloading the sleds as the cook started on dinner. King Borislav then did something I never would have suspected. He transformed in front of me. It privileged me to meet Borislav when I wrote a small piece on 'The Tracking Masters of the North' a few years back. It shocked me to discover he was a shapeshifter. I was just unprepared this time for the change when the Great Winter Wolf — a legend among humans — towered over me in his majesty. Brilliant grey and white fur with steel-blue eyes. His red stained lips curled and gave a short growl, lifting a front leg in my direction. The command was unmistakable, 'Get on'.

What do you do when a giant wolf commands you to get on its back? You obey.

He leapt through the narrow paths as I clung tightly to his back, locking my cybernetic arm so I wouldn't fall off. I made a mental note to return to Ambasere soon and start a book on the White Wolf.

He brought me to the mouth of a cave...a single path etched in stone, surrounded by what resembled kutollum stonework. Borislav transformed back into his human form, taking the lead while I popped my mechanical hand back to use my excavation light down the hole. The path led us deep into the earth, where I mistook the catacombs for constructing Kutollum stonework.

As we descended, King Borislav rumbled, 'I think you won't soon forget Vankiläsä.' He then shared the story of the cave's discovery.

In the early days of his father's kingdom, villages had to deal with attacks from wolves and bears. Slaughtering livestock, they'd even carry off the unattended young of the village. A hunting party had been tracking a beast for days and mistook the entrance for a bear's cave. The party of warriors entered with spears and torches, only to discover the bones of hundreds of humans. Rows of contorted human bones awaited them, with a few already decayed to the bone, but most frozen and preserved after death.

His timing was perfect. For just as he finished speaking, I could look around and see for myself what they saw. It was just as King Borislav had said. But there was more. Most had a round symbol carved into the stone above their heads. These had similar symbols burned into their bodies. In the deepest reaches of the cave, the skeletons became much larger; the teeth were sharp and jagged. Vallen. ...all in the same contorted shapes and lying under symbols etched in the walls.

I had examined the carvings and brands, but didn't recognize any of the symbols. I couldn't recognize any of the symbols in these carvings and brands, which was puzzling because I can identify various forms of magic. These symbols didn't fit any established patterns I knew of.

Borislav then pulled from his tunic a scroll of cloth

and handed it to me. The scroll of cloth that Borislav handed to me had writing stitched on it, which is his people's way of preserving older records. He said they had rewritten it from scrolls found at this site. The language was Baiūmen and revealed that these were not tombs at all...but cells. The prisoners, who were the foulest of evil-doers, were sentenced to death. To be used in an experiment sanctioned by High King Gaston when Andilain was a nation of itself.

The bodies were abandoned, and the Ambasere hunters reported their findings back to Borislav's father. The cave remained a well-guarded secret, kept from any records. They feared King Alik and his people being accused of some unspeakable crime against their own race.

As a fishis of the Gnome Nation, I documented and time stamped the ruins and ancient shackles. I can estimate that the construction took place between 6011s and 6014s. This happened long before Andilain divided and Borislav's father ruled his own people.

The cloth holds record of a human mägo and Kutollum miners using prisoners sentenced to death to work the mines. Vankiläsä means 'prison of the damned'.

Setting the cloth scroll down on the table, I can't stop staring at the letters in front of me.

Ah-hah. I found you.

I have walked the path of Eamon, the mägo clerk.

I have seen the works of his hands, or at least the effects of his experiments.

And now you are going to Holääfeldi.

CHAPTER 12
LETTER ELEVEN

My Beloved Ethany,

I have confined myself to my quarters. You cannot possibly understand the anger and disappointment I have felt. And I cannot convey it on parchment. What a waste of our time together. If all along I was to die an untimely death, I would rather have spent my last years and days with you and the girls. What a waste. A cruel and point-less waste.

Day 1006. It won't work. Shiro and I have used up all the Vallen slaves captured in battle. No matter how we try, there is not enough life force, even within a giant vallen, to satisfy the requirements to bind the Dark Lord. It simply cannot be done.

But this is not all. The seals are too fragile. Even the most basic of magic can sever the binding of a rune.

Our efforts have been futile, and I have wasted my life. My work has been in vain.

I have failed.
-Eamon

There it is in writing. '...to bind the Dark Lord.' This is the history of the Demoni Vankil. From Eamon I now know that it used rune magic—but I'm not exactly sure how and that it required the combining of the Seven Disciplines.

I could kick myself. Decades I have searched. These letters have been hidden for *decades*. **DECADES**!!

The story I have sought to tell more than any other... staring me in the face!

Once and for all, Höbin Luckyfeller will put the fables and assumptions to rest with cold, hard facts!

I found myself cheering him on.

Don't give up yet.
You are so close.
Tell me more.

CHAPTER 13
LETTER TWELVE

My Beloved Ethany,

King Kimmeldell brought me a visitor today. It was Charles. It seems strange to me - his visits. I am questioning what his part is in all of this. I was, however, looking forward to seeing a friendly face.

But that is not what I saw. In fact, I may have not recognized him in another setting. His hair, which was once neatly trimmed, is now shaggy and unkempt, and his face, which was once handsome, is now scarred, creased, and unshaven. Even his eyes had a fire in them that made him look stern. Could these be the effects of fighting on the front lines of this war since I saw him last? He, we both, have aged a great deal.

Charles related to me impassioned, the conditions of the war, the devastation and death plaguing the land. Not a single village or city to the south has survived. Mahan now controls Tämä-Un and the Prime Gate.

It will surprise you to hear what happened next, my dear. For you probably believe it isn't in either of our nature.

We contended bitterly against one another.

Charles has been most unkind about my completing this work and the time it has taken. He kept repeating that it would work... and that I must make it work. I tried to explain the limitations of the runes, but he won't listen to reason. He became red faced in his anger, and raising his voice to me said my results were unacceptable and my attitude deplorable.

His judgements of me are unforgivable, for I, too, as you know, have suffered and sacrificed a great deal. I can do nothing when I have nothing!

They will not hold me responsible for this failure.

He then tried to make me swear I would not give until I had succeeded.

But I would not.

Maybe I overreacted, being frustrated over the current state of this work and he being worn out from his labors. I know not. Whatever the cause, he's gone now.

Maybe my part is over and I will come home soon.

All my love,
Eamon

P.S. Gratefully, Charles had not left. He is the last person I want to be at odds with.

It appears he took my words to heart and has been in council with King Kimmeldell.

Charles announced he believed the Kutollum possessed the answer to our problem. And then the dwarf King reverently placed a jeweled case before me, which made me leery.

Ethany, it was a Lanthya! A most prized possession of this race and King Kimmeldell gingerly handed me the shard to use with the runes. He assured me that no less a cause could have compelled his people to part with it.

At first touch, I could feel the power emanating from it, even though it was smaller than the other crystals we have been using. I wonder also if he knew that if the Lanthya had enough life force, it would never return to his keeping.

We would still need two more.

How can we accomplish such a feat? I felt sorry for that but chose not to mention it.

I gave the shard to Shiro for study and to practice upon and we resumed our experiments the following day. Shiro shouted with excitement when he channeled the energy from the crystal into the seal of the rune. There was no limit to its power! We created and activated four insignificant runes, investing none of our time...

Charles may have saved us all.

There are no historical records on the Lanthya, even though historians know they exist. I have seen one myself.

Legend says the Lanthya fell from the skies, a gift from the Gods. An actual piece of their own home world, intelligent and filled with wisdom, sent to teach us and help us.

Unfortunately, the people of the Elämä bickered and fought over who was to 'own' the Lanthya and bloodshed ensued. So the Lanthya split herself into twelve lesser pieces—eleven shards and a 'heart stone', to be shared as a gift to all people. One piece to each organized 'clan'.

This is when the first Mahan appeared, seeking to obtain the shards—and use them to bring all people under his dominion. As the wars grew, Mahan gained several of the shards and became nearly invincible—drawing on the unlimited life force to power his magic.

But the intelligence of the Lanthya had remained in the 'heart stone'. The Ithari, she called herself. She chose a humble boy among the people to be her Hero. To be the one she would grant all her power for his service to the people. He was to be the warrior against the forces of darkness and to defeat the Dark Lord Mahan.

It was the last battle between the Hero and Mahan which caused the Great Sundering. It tore the world apart, sending lands across the waters and dividing each race.

CHAPTER 14
LETTER THIRTEEN

My Beloved Ethany,

I awoke this morning to shouts echoing through the halls of Holääfeldi. Dwarven criers bellowing "High King Gaston is dead and Mahan is captured."

Upon further investigation, I am told that the Omethiä, the Head Speaker of the Evolu, and Lord Soturi of the Nocturi, have also fallen.

King Kimmeldell the Bold, even now, clings to life, having received great wounds in the Battle of Northridge against the Vallen hordes. They dispatched the finest healers in Holääfeldi in haste, but there was little hope of arriving in time.

Had the dwarves not dismantled their own Prime Gate during the war, this would not have been a concern.

The victory is not yet full enough to outweigh the sorrow and devastation that has settled down upon these people. The dark cloud of grief engulfs them. And I mourn with them. I should never want to forget the moans and sobs of a people in despair when the savagery of war robs them of loved ones in open mockery.

The pains in my chest have become unbearable.

Ethany, I feel I am responsible for their loss. How can I not feel guilty when they sacrificed their lives for me to finish this work?

My only consolation is that it is done. Oh, that you could hear me cry to the mountains—'I am done! You may have no more blood!'

After 1402 days since I left you and the girls, do I dare hope that this war is finally over? I have been praying for years for the end to come, and so much has been lost! Yet,

I am reassured it is true—my time has finally come.

I know now you would not recognize me, my love, for I am nothing but a shadow of my former self. My mind may burn with the power of rune knowledge, but my body has all but withered away in my dedication to this task. Only now do I understand. The ancient Runelords of folklore did not allow this magic to fade into myth. It consumed them until there was nothing left of them.

I have perfected the runes, and everything is in order. I am ready.

Three runes.

One to bind the tongue and one to bind the body. It shall be impossible for the Dark Lord to weave his spells.

The third is special. It will bind him to Unrest itself, forged from the ore of that frozen world...forcing that immortal damnation to exist in a hell of living death.

I have named it Demoni Vankil, the Devils Prison.

I have separated the seals from the marks. If the seals cannot be found, they cannot be broken. We have only to place the marks upon him and it will be done.

I leave this very night for Castle Andilain with a branch of Kimmeldell's personal guard to watch over me and preserve my life. Four of the three newly cast Runelords, only I remain to speak the incantations. We will travel light and fast to the capital for the ritual. I have the privilege of delivering the final blow. This irrevocable act holds my loathing, my pain, my hatred...and my revenge.

My warm clothing is worn through. They have given me a red cloak to keep me warm. I wish I could travel to Andilain by the Prime Gate, that my tasks may be done and I can return home.

Tell the girls it won't be much longer. Will you wait for me?

All my love,
Eamon

Demoni Vankil—*the Devil's Prison.*

Ahem—Yeah.

That was my second guess.

Eager to know of the end, I unfolded the last letter.

CHAPTER 15
LETTER FOURTEEN

My Beloved Ethany,

It is done.

There is nothing left for me here and I am free to go.

I have lived a lifetime without you these four years. A life I would wish upon no man, nor ask any heart to endure, though I have few regrets.

In the time I have labored, I have learned an important lesson.

Though we have bound the Dark Lord and cast him out from among us, darkness will return. It is a heavy blow to a man's greatest work to know it is for naught. We will forever be vulnerable to the weaknesses in

our own hearts and our selfish desires.
Power, money, lusts of the flesh and any
other desire which takes a man, a family, a
village or a nation from peace or freedom.

It is the sword of tyranny and the
enemy of all.

For until men desire to control their own
passions, evil roots itself in their hearts and
darkness will rise again.

I am certain of this.

Mahan will return, though it be by
another name.

Such is the war of mankind.
My deed is done. I am consumed.
I am coming home.

All my love,
Eamon

That is the end of the letters. But not a satisfactory end of the story for me.

I want to know the details of the Demoni Vankil.

I wish someone had provided solid proof of how this was done, but the records are tainted. Each race involved in the conflict has their own version of the story.

They claim that their race defeated and bound the Dark Lord, except for the Iskäri.

The Evolu used the power of the elements to send the dark army fleeing and then cast a great sleep upon Mahan.

The Nocturi destroyed the dark armies with such power that Mahan begged for mercy.

Humans say Gaston challenged Mahan openly. That his archers pierced the Dark Lord with arrows to the extent it weakened him enough that the mägo Orders could use befuddlement and sleep charms on him.

The Kutollum say King Kimmeldell and his legion of dwarves decimated the dark army and bound Mahan in chains of enchanted metal.

...but the greatest version was from *my* people.

They claim to have annihilated the dark army with Gnome-powered robots and kept Mahan sedated by an electric choke-collar.

Yeah—the Gnomes didn't **have** technology yet... and they didn't even FIGHT in the war!

However, the accounts are straightforward that the Kings of all four races gave their lives to defeat Mahan and his army upon the fields of Andilain. That's in the

Book of Four Kings.

What happened to Eamon?

I don't think they would rebuke me for saying this man is one of the greatest mägo in history. Yet, according to prominent records, he doesn't exist?!?

After what he accomplished, I'm surprised.

Did nobody think that they should write this down? To remember?

Did he go to Bailish to meet his family?

No. Somewhere along this trail I read of Bailish being overcome.

Apparently he met up with Ethany and the children, because I found her letters and Hammel's puzzle box in the kirk.

Where's my happy ending?

Full and satisfied?

Neat and tidy?

Nope.

I am going to Andilain.

CHAPTER 16
HÖBINS LAST DISCOVERY

These letters sent me to far lands over the course of two years, putting together one of the greatest puzzles in my career.

I grew very fond of this Eamon, from Tildan. In the end, I travelled to Andilain once more and gained permission directly from King Robert III to study the records of the Church.

I had missed something.

I took a few days to remember that the Church requested me to supervise a kirk excavation site decades ago. I forgot to access the most obvious resources available to me: the Brotherhood. The records are independent from the rest of the world and protected by the power of the crown.

It was the law that for anyone condemned to die, a

priest of the Brotherhood would be present to be a witness and record all that was done.

Mahan did not die, but he was being condemned... which meant there was most likely a priest present and recording during the event.

I was feeling embarrassed.

Could it actually be this simple? To quench the burning desire to know how Mahan, the greatest evil of all, had been bound and exiled. And to piece together the fragments of a life which had become a friend to me. A friend by the name of Eamon.

Brother Owens' journal states:

"Old age has come too soon for me. I fear that this request of Queen Älodiä may be my last opportunity to serve her. Alas, King Gaston is dead. I administered to his burial myself. I am old and worn and unable to be the man I once was, but still I stand by our Queen in this mournful hour in defiance of darkness."

"They gathered us around the Prime Gate in Andilain. Being created first it is the strongest. There are none here who are unnecessary to the ritual. Mahan is in the center of the platform. None may stand near the prisoner, only the Gnolaum and the mägo, exerting their powers to keep the devil quiet and still."

"There is an older man, pale, withered and hunched in a red robe, working with the Kutollum in stoking a

fire just aside the steps of the Gate. There are three irons in the fire. We wait in hushed silence for the man in red to begin."

"The Dark Lord struggles and cries out to the Gnolaum, 'Would you curse a wayward friend?'"

"I do not understand, but it took aback the Gnolaum as the Dark Lord laughs."

"The man in red looked to me as he took one iron from the fire. 'I am ready.'"

"I ask if he would like to have his name recorded. He said 'no'."

"Two Kutollum take the other irons from the fire and we follow the man in red up the stairs and to the devil's side. He examines the iron in his hands and then leans down to the devil's ear and I am forced to follow."

"'For this moment, I have sacrificed all I have ever had to give.' And without hesitation, he thrust the burning iron into the devil's forehead, chanting words I cannot recall or identify."

"The hysterical laughter turns to screams as the man in red leans in hard. A scream which rends the very fabric of nature. I can smell the stench of burning flesh."

"Trees within the courtyard split in twain and the ground rocks and trembles. The Gnolaum calls out to the man in red but he was unmoving. I question if this is really necessary. He only smiles as he pulls the iron from the wound, casts it aside and holds out an open hand to the Kutollum."

"I am stunned to see the flesh completely burned away, and the marks seared into bone."

"The Dark Lord's screams grow with each touch until I fear the world will rip asunder. Three times is the devil branded thus, but as the third mark penetrates the devil's flesh, silence falls upon us. The ground is still. Though evil thrashes, eyes wide in pain and terror, he cannot scream."

"The Prime Gate is opened when the Gnolaum speaks the words. Through the portal, I can see only darkness. The devil's body rises from the altar, an invisible force pulling him violently into the void, still restrained by chains."

"The man in red whispers so only the devil and I can hear: 'From darkness you came, to darkness you will return.'"

"With a snap of his fingers, the chains of the altar release their captive. They cast the contorted body of Mahan into the darkness, his eyes wide with a terror I cannot even imagine."

"The Gnolaum closes the gate, and all is silent. There are no cheers, no laughter, not a sound of nature."

"We have ended the war, and we have defeated the enemy. I turned to speak peace unto the man in *red, but he was walking away. I never saw him again."*

So where did Eamon go?

I could only assume to find Ethany and the children, which would lead to the kirk excavation.

It wasn't long before I located the personal journal of the priest of the kirk in question. There was a note on the box from the Church that caught my eye:

"Contents: Journal of Brother Drydan, Book of Songs, Laws of The Brotherhood, ...one red puzzle box (missing)"

Woops.

Brother Drydan.

He seemed determined to have his journals endure. I say this because they committed none of his records to paper but on brass sheets bound by simple metal rings.

Interesting, maybe clever. Probably a former blacksmith.

Anyway, I didn't find what I thought I would.

"An old man, soaked and shivering in dirty red robes, was turned face down and nearly frozen to death, not more than a hundred feet from my doorstep."

"Oh, that I would have heard him! Seen him! I

could have saved him. Throughout the night, I prayed and worked to break his fever, but it would not. Death was determined to have him. May the Gods bless his soul for the sufferings he must have endured along this long road alone and away from his loved ones."

"It is rarely that circumstances prevent me from keeping my vow, for I know not his name and in this I am tormented. He clung to a small red box as if his soul were contained, and only whispered 'Ethany' from his lips."

"So I have done what I can. His body was prepared and buried, but not without a stone. I cannot bear to lay him to rest without a name, and so I place upon his stone, 'He who loves Ethany' in the hope that the Gods will have mercy on his soul...and mine."

"I tried to open the box he clung to, but was unable. I can hear the contents inside, and so I will send it on to those wiser than I to discover its fate."

That was it. The end of the path.

Eamon was alone in the end and had the box and was the one who ended up at the kirk.

Before I returned home, I traveled south to the original excavation site. The hole where we dug was now a fishing pond, filled in by the overflow from the river. There were no gravestones to look at, so I walked the land for a spell and ended up resting under a large cottonwood tree, the red puzzle box turning in my hands. This was a disturbing end. My hands absent-mindedly slid the pieces randomly across the surface.

The bottom of the box popped open.

...there was a locket, two small bracelets and a folded, fragile letter.

It had the red wax stains of a royal seal.

EPILOGUE

FROM HER ROYAL HIGHNESS,
LADY ÄLODIÄ, QUEEN OF
ANDILAIN

My dearest Eamon,

It is with a heavy heart that I send this letter. For I gave you my solemn vow to keep your wife and daughters safe from the darkness plaguing this land, and I have failed you.

Guards escorted your wife and daughters from their home just days after you departed the Castle for Vankiläsä. They took them to our stronghold in Bailish, as I had promised. Ethany was accepted into Lord Brahms' care and, at my request, given a home and position in his household. He committed to watch over her and the children personally.

We could not have foreseen what would shortly come.

They have not invaded the Eastern shores in the history this nation. Within a fortnight, Bailish was overrun by Mahan's forces. We were betrayed by Ogriel among our own people. They immediately dispatched a rider for reinforcements from the capital, which were granted in haste, but our forces were too late.

The stronghold and village had been laid waste. They discovered Lord Brahms' armored caravan ten miles west of the stronghold.

We found the bodies of your wife and daughters among those soldiers trying to defend them. Lord Brahm perished at the base of the stronghold's gate, surrounded by the bodies of his faithful men, many wounds piercing his body.

High Lord Gastons' army engaged the enemy in the forests of Whitewater the following morning. We destroyed them from the face of the land, their bodies denied burial and burned.

We mourn your loss, Eamon.

Words cannot express our sorrow for your family and for our failure. I have tended to the ceremonial needs of your loved ones, my friend. I have laid them to rest among the Kings and Queens of Andilain, their bodies prepared by my own hands.

There were two letters discovered, which your love kept close to her breast while you were apart. A testament of her devotion to you, I have no doubt.

These I return to you, along with her locket and two bracelets we found upon the wrists of your beloved children. May they rest in the sweet company of loved ones who have gone before them.

Eamon, we pray you will be strong and ever determined to aid us in ridding our land of the enemy. Let not the pain and sacrifice of your loved ones be in vain. Avenge them and every other family Mahan has taken.

The crown will ever be mindful of your sacrifice and your service, my friend. If you have need of anything, you have only to ask. Our love, support and blessings are forever with you until our journey's end.

With deepest respect and admiration,
Lady Älodiä
Queen of Andilain

GET EARLY ACCESS
BOOKS, COMICS, PODCASTS,
EVEN ARTWORK,...DIRECTLY
FROM THE AUTHOR.

LifeOfFiction.com offers early access for just $7 a month. Members get each and every chapter written, as they are written, sent directly to their email inbox.

Every chapter, podcast episodes, all the artwork, and if you want even more, you have complete access to the *archives*. Join conversations and share what you think directly with the author!

Best part is, if you don't mind *telling other readers* about **Life of Fiction**, you can earn a subscription instead.

We also provide 'Hardship Scholarships' for military, first responders, and yes...even homeschoolers. If you cannot afford $7 a month, just contact us at lifeoffic tion@substack.com. We can get you a coupon code, depending upon your need and circumstances.

Let us help feed your fiction-addiction.

Visit us at LifeOfFiction.com.

ABOUT THE AUTHOR

HÖBIN LUCKYFELLER IS WHAT people refer to as a *field-scribe-historian* (or *fishis* for short), hence the term—*field work is for the fishis*. He specializes in acquiring unique information, not readily available to a 'normal' historian (that means the yahoo's who still write with pen and paper instead of using a laptop).

The fact is, he's famous for one special reason: *He's gone where no Gnome has gone before.*

Höbin's qualifications include studying under the renown scribe and botanist **Bigsby Bumblebutt,** earning his Field Degree from Clockworks Academy. After the Gate War, he requested Isle-Leave from the Government Faction and got his black card, taking his surviving two children—Alhannah and Green with him on remote field assignments. Since then he's earned a Doctorate in both *field analytics, animal linguistics* and graduated as a *Qualified Crocodile* through the human performance mastery program under the tutelage of Roger M Anthony.

He is proficient in *arcane analysis, magic fundamentals* and *advanced cybernetic adaptation and engineering*. Höbin also make a mean quiche and an impressive lemon sorbet.

This is his first **public** release of knowledge, which he hopes to be a success for two important reasons: One, because you have a right to know the truth about Elämä and all that pertains to it, and; Two, ...he needs drinking money.

ABOUT THE PUBLISHER

JAIME BUCKLEY IS A storyteller, illustrator, and an editor at Perspicacious Publishing. When he's not engaged in hunting monsters, acting as a survival flotation device or a master sliver-picker-outer (just ask his little kids), he's also a cartoonist, game creator, blogger, podcaster and avid teacher.

Jaime is known for his *Chronicles of a Hero* series, his Advanced WORLDBUILDING guide, and his dynamic BOUNDLESS Journal assisting writers in building fictional worlds faster, easier and in more detail than ever before. What he is *best* known for, however, is catering to and pampering his exclusive readers through LifeOfFiction.com, sharing early access to his new fictional works.

He lives in the Rocky Mountains with his family and loves communicating with readers from all over the world.

www.ingramcontent.com/pod-product-compliance
Lightning Source LLC
Chambersburg PA
CBHW052141220626
47052CB00005B/1143